For Shelley—
always my sister, a lovely carnation.
—N.T.

For my mom, Elena—
I wish you could have seen me bloom.
—A.P.

Planted with Love
Growing into a Family

WRITTEN BY
Natasha Tripplett

ILLUSTRATED BY
Adriana Predoi

Lamar steps out of the car and looks at all the plants.

"What a mess," he mumbles.

In his new room, Lamar unpacks his bag.

"Do you want to see the garden?" his new foster mother asks. Lamar shakes his head.

He watches from the window.

She weeds.

She waters.

She waits.

Her colorful gloves dig in the dirt.

The kids in the last foster home called him dirty.

A lonely wilderness of shame spreads inside him.

He knows he won't be here for long.

"Do you want to see the garden?" she asks again.

Lamar shakes his head.

Seven days watching from the window.

She digs.
  She pulls.
    She waters.
      She sings.

She looks up at the window and waves. Lamar turns away.

One day he watches from the doorway.

She smiles and beckons him over.

"Come see the seedlings. They just sprouted today."

With cautious curiosity, Lamar steps outside.

Small shoots peek through the dirt.

He watches as she tenderly tucks the soil in around them.

"What's your favorite color?" she asks.

"Blue," he says confidently.

Blue for the pen his dad gave him.

Together, they weed.
Together, they water.
Together, they wait.

Lamar listens to her talk about planting flowers with her mother every year. A pang of envy pricks his heart.

Kids like him don't even stay in the same place year after year.

Are these flowers more important than me? Lamar wonders.

His sadness grows into anger.

He weeds.

He waters.

He waits.

Now I've really made a mess. Is it time to pack?
A pit of guilt swells inside him.

He watches from the window.

She sighs.

She rakes.

She pauses.

She smiles.

She looks up at the window and waves him down.

Lamar's heart pounds as he steps outside.

Is she going to yell?

"Look. The garden is still intact." She points to the little bud.

"All we need is one plant to make a garden," she assures him.

She hands him his gardening gloves.

Together, they plant.

Together, they water.

Together, they wait.

Lamar feels a twinge of hope.

"Daisies are perennials. They flower year after year," she says.

"Petunias are annuals. They need to be replanted every year."

Lamar thinks about all the times he's had to start over.

Weighed down by memories, he asks, "Am I an annual?"

He sobs.

She hugs.

He worries.

She whispers.

"You are a perennial.
You are wanted.
You are planted.
You are loved."

Lamar puts away his suitcase.

He dreams.

He grows.

He blooms.

Text copyright © 2025 by Natasha Tripplett
Cover art and interior illustrations
copyright © 2025 by Adriana Predoi

All rights reserved.

Published in the United States by WaterBrook,
an imprint of Random House,
a division of Penguin Random House LLC.

WATERBROOK and its colophon are registered
trademarks of Penguin Random House LLC.

ISBN 978-0-593-58076-9
Ebook ISBN 978-0-593-58077-6

The Library of Congress catalog record is
available at https://lccn.loc.gov/2022039116.

Printed in China

waterbrookmultnomah.com

9 8 7 6 5 4 3 2 1

First Edition

Book and cover design by Monique Sterling

Most WaterBrook books are available at special quantity discounts for bulk purchase for premiums, fundraising, and corporate and educational needs by organizations, churches, and businesses. Special books or book excerpts also can be created to fit specific needs. For details, contact specialmarketscms@penguinrandomhouse.com.